D1297903

THE HAPPY HUNTER

by Roger Duvoisin

ENCHANTED LION BOOKS
NEW YORK

The Happy Hunter

Mr. Bobbin
lived in a little house at the edge of the forest.
He loved to sit on the bench by his door
and smoke his pipe while he watched the hills,
the sky, and the wild animals.

When the forest turned yellow
he watched the hunters go by in their
big yellow caps and big yellow coats,
big black boots with yellow stockings,
big brown belts with rows of cartridges,
big shiny guns under their arms.
They looked like knights in armor as they went in search
of little rabbits, partridges and pheasants.

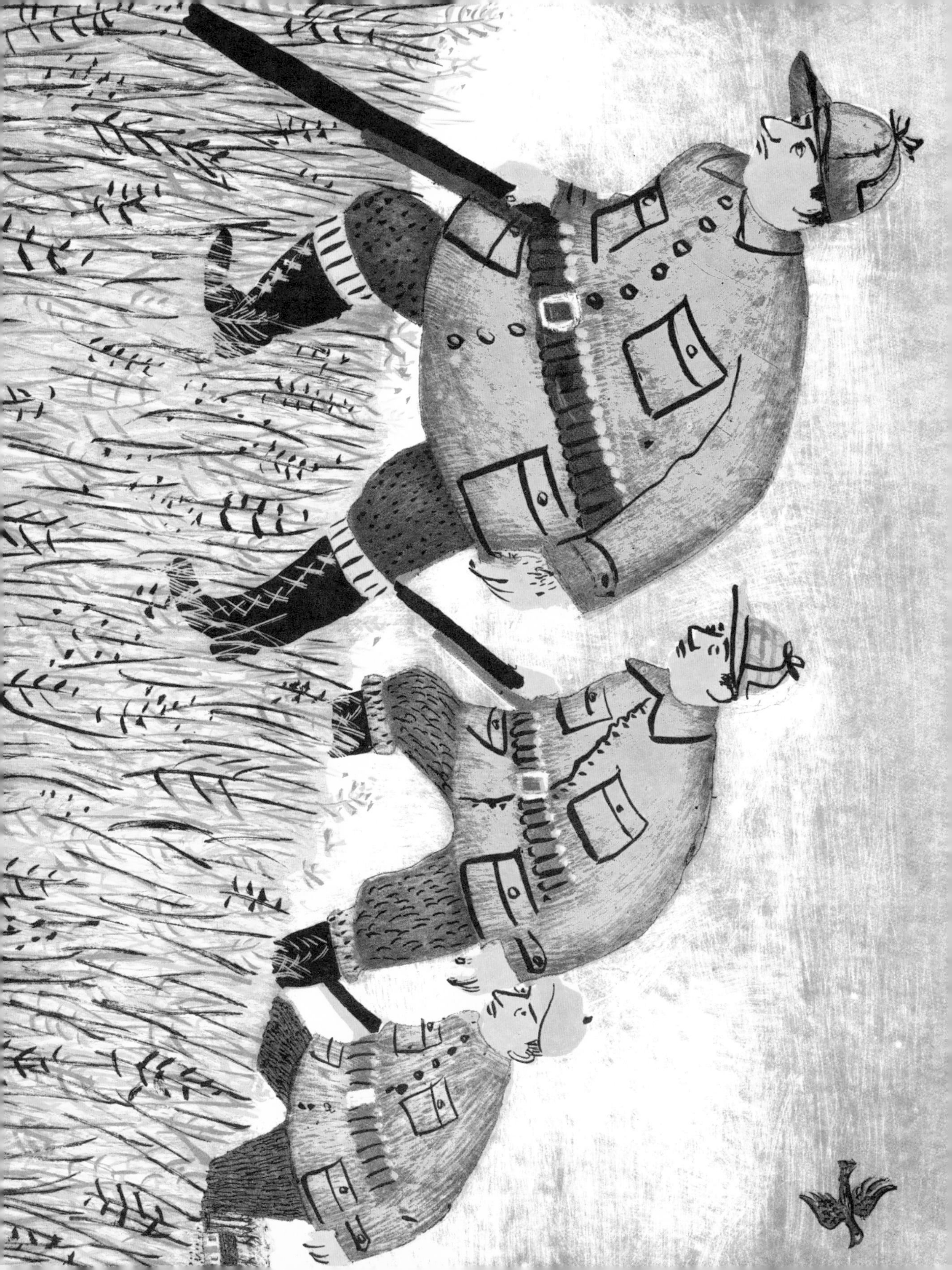

"It must be nice," thought Mr. Bobbin,
blowing a cloud of smoke from his pipe,
"to look so big and bold and to walk through the forest,
across fields, up the hills and down the valleys.
It would be nice to have a fine gun to clean and polish."
So, Mr. Bobbin bought himself

a big yellow cap and a big yellow coat,
big black boots with yellow stockings,
a big brown belt with rows of cartridges,
a big gun to carry under his arm.

And Mr. Bobbin went hunting.

When Mr. Bobbin saw a little rabbit
chewing dried grass behind a clump of weeds,
he raised his gun and peeped through the sight
and peeped . . . and peeped . . .   . . . and peeped,
and then he put his gun down and coughed, "Hm . . . hm . . . hm."
The rabbit looked up and said, "Heavens, a hunter!"
And in three strides he was off in the tall grass.
"That was a quick little rabbit," said Mr. Bobbin with a smile
and he wiped his shiny gun with his handkerchief.

When Mr. Bobbin saw a squirrel
cracking a nut on a stone,
he crouched behind a honeysuckle
with his fine gun up to his eye, and
he aimed . . . and aimed . . .   . . . just aimed,
and then he sang a little tune: “De-dum, de-dum.”
The squirrel dropped his nut and said,
“Whoops, a hunter hunting.” In one jump he was up a tree.
“A clever little squirrel,” said Mr. Bobbin
and he sat down for a picnic lunch.

Mr. Bobbin came home late that evening.
He was tired but happy.
“Hunting is not quite what I thought,” he said.
“But still, it was a lovely hunting day.
I had a nice walk through the fields.”
And he polished his fine gun and went to bed,
after a good meal of Boston beans and tea.

When Mr. Bobbin went hunting next time,
he saw a pheasant picking grapes in the wood.
He hid behind a rock and held up his polished gun
very still . . . very still . . . . . . just very still,
and then he whistled, "SSSS . . . SSS . . . SSSSS."
"Oh, dear me!" shrieked the pheasant, "a hunter with a gun."
And with heavy wingbeats he flew off among the trees.
"That was a specially beautiful bird but a noisy one,"
said Mr. Bobbin happily and he picked up a feather
to stick in his cap.

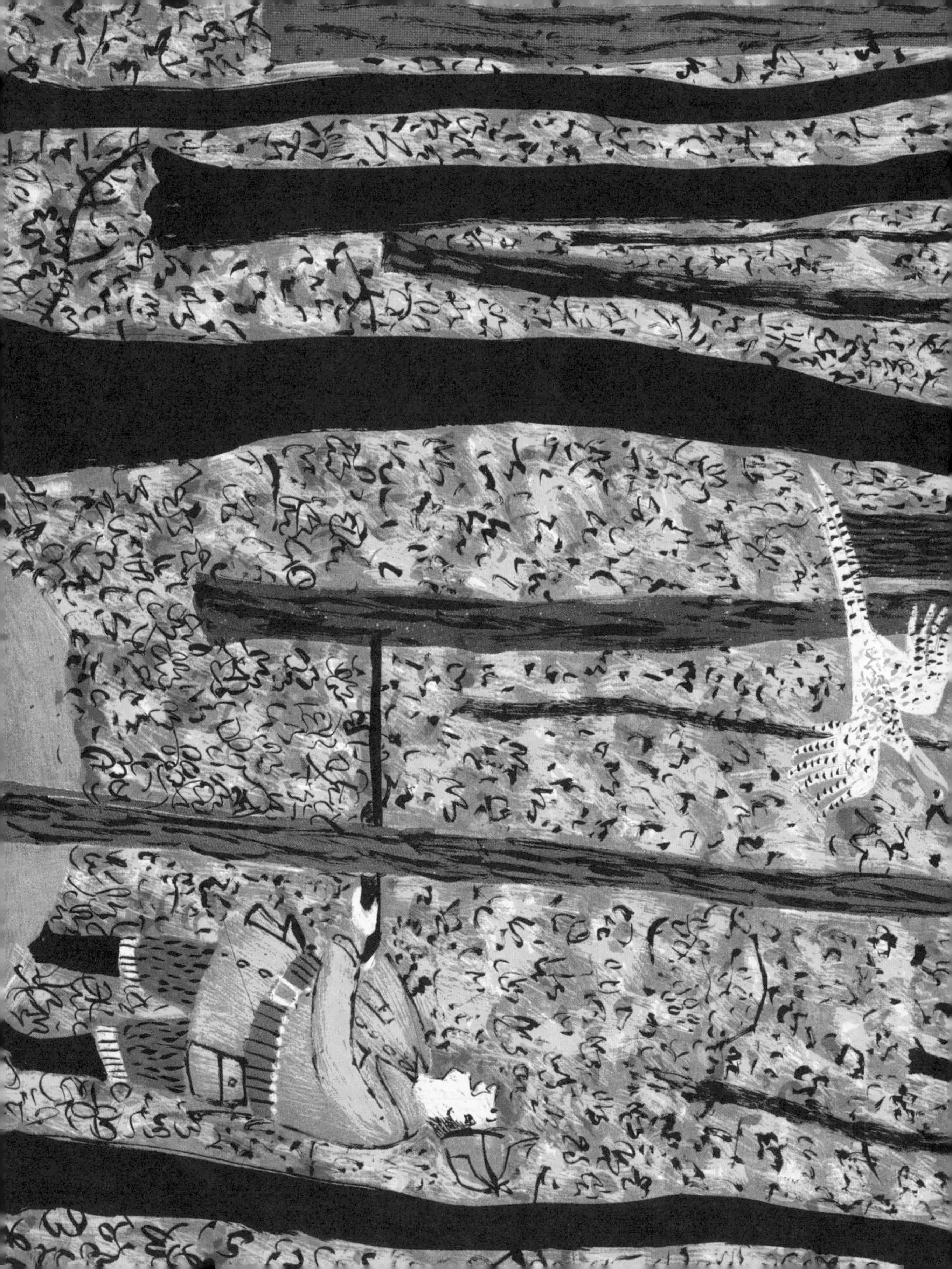

When Mr. Bobbin saw a little duck
swallowing a bug by the green pond in the valley,
he lay down with his gun behind a fallen tree
and watched . . . and watched . . . . . . just watched,
and then he took out his handkerchief and blew his nose.
"Quack, quack, quack," cried the little duck,
choking on a bug, "a hunter! Let's not tarry here."
And with a bow, he dived into the pond.
"Ducks are lovely birds," said Mr. Bobbin, lighting his pipe.

Mr. Bobbin was happier than ever
when he went home that night. “Hunting is nice,” he said.
“I had a wonderful walk down the valley.”
He polished his shiny gun
and ate a hearty meal of pancakes and milk.

When the frost was in the air next year,
Mr. Bobbin went hunting again.
He saw a fox sunning himself atop a stone wall
and he leaned against a tree to hold his gun
steady . . . very steady . . .   . . . very steady,
and then he sneezed: "Atchumm! Atchuuummmm!"
"Well," said the fox, looking sideways, "if it isn't Mr. Bobbin
with his shiny gun." And he yawned and went to sleep.
"That's the fattest, foxiest fox of the forest,"
said Mr. Bobbin, very pleased with the encounter.

When Mr. Bobbin saw an opossum munching crab apples
at the edge of the stream, he propped himself
against an old fence and shouldered his shiny gun
gently . . . carefully . . . . . . very carefully,
and suddenly slapped his cheek, "Ouch, a bee stung me."
"Bah," said the opossum, too busy to look up,
"here comes Mr. Bobbin. I wonder why he takes his gun
when he goes hunting."
And he went on picking the choicest apples.
"That's a wise opossum," said Mr. Bobbin.
"He eats well before winter comes."

"Well," said Mr. Bobbin, going home that night,
"that was another beautiful hunting day.
I had a lovely walk through the forest." And he put away
his big yellow cap and his big yellow coat,
his big black boots with yellow stockings,
his big brown belt with rows of cartridges,
and his big shiny gun.
Then he had a delicious meal
of noodles, applesauce, and hot chocolate.

Every year for many years when the leaves turned yellow,
Mr. Bobbin went hunting
through the forest, across the fields, and up the hills.
He knew all the woods and the streams, and the animals.
But one year he found it was too hard to walk all day with
his big yellow cap and big yellow coat,
his big black boots with yellow stockings,
his big brown belt with rows of cartridges,
his big shiny gun under his arm.
Perhaps Mr. Bobbin had become too old.
He was very sad.

Now all the animals wondered what had become of Mr. Bobbin.
"Why doesn't he hunt anymore?" asked the duck. "I miss him so."
"Perhaps he has moved away," said the rabbit.
"Perhaps he is sick," said the pheasant.
"I'll tell you," said the fox.
"Mr. Bobbin has become too old to hunt.
He just sits and smokes his pipe on the bench by his door."
"Then let's visit him," said the bear.

So, the bear, the deer and the fox, the raccoon, the rabbit, the woodchuck, the squirrel and the opossum, the pheasant, the partridge and the quail, came in the afternoons to sit with Mr. Bobbin by the door of his little house.

So, the years were still full of happy days for Mr. Bobbin.

Designed by Roger Duvoisin
Set in Caslon 540

www.enchantedlion.com

First reprint edition published in 2016 by Enchanted Lion Books,
351 Van Brunt Street, Brooklyn, NY 11231

Originally published in 1961 by Lothrop, Lee & Shepard.

A CIP record is on file with the Library of Congress. ISBN 978-1-59270-205-3

Color restoration and layout: Marc Drumwright

Printed in China in May 2016 by RR Donnelley Asia Printing Solutions Ltd.

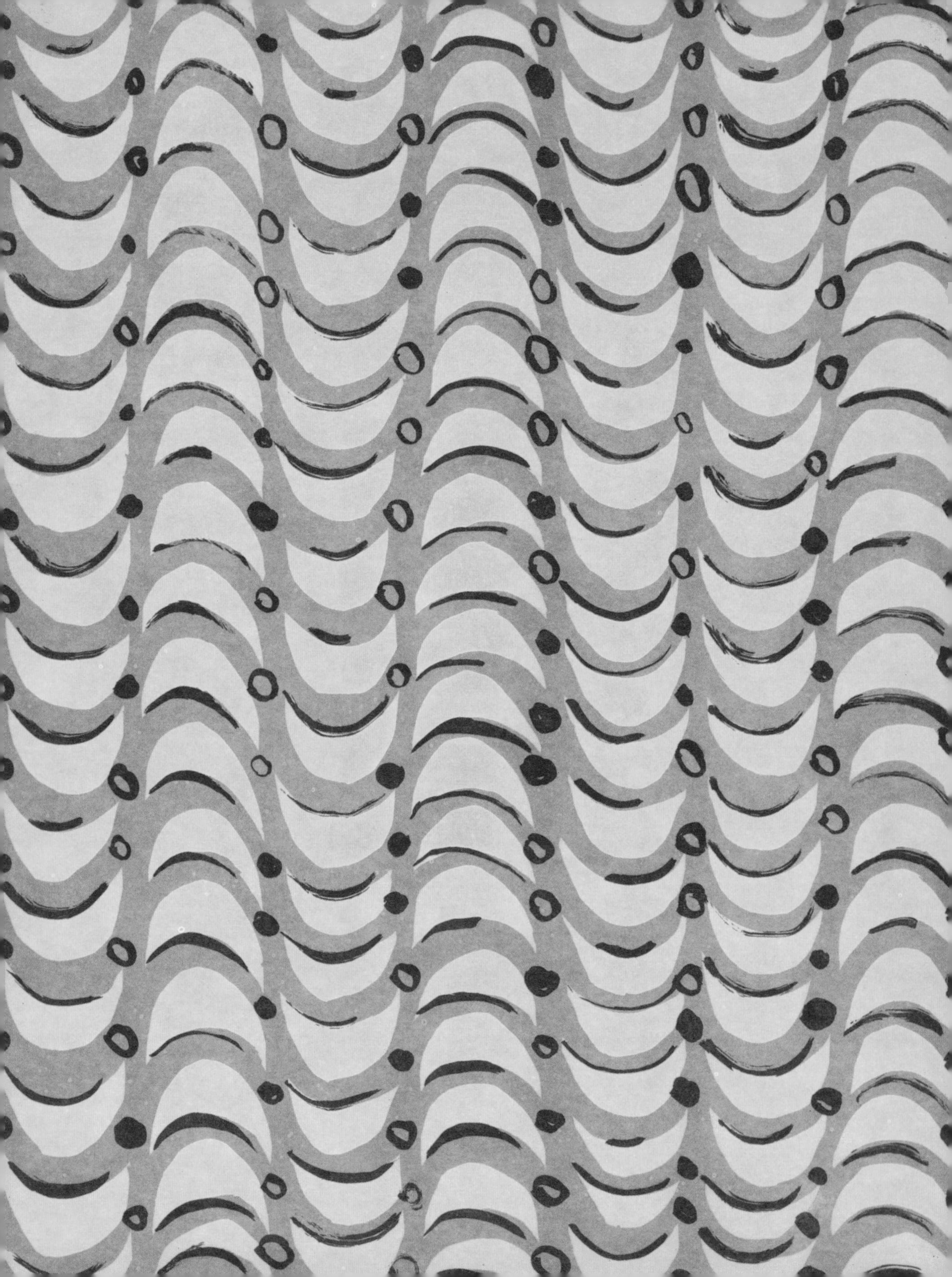